Loose Connections

Published by Accent Press Ltd – 2010

ISBN 9781907016394

The Quick Reads project in Wales is a joint venture between Basic Skills Cymru and the Welsh Books Council. Titles are funded through Basic Skills Cymru as part of the National Basic Skills Strategy for Wales on behalf of the Welsh Assembly Government.

Printed and bound in the UK

Cover Design by Red Dot Design

CYNGOR LLYFRAU CYMRU
WELSH BOOKS COUNCIL

Noddir gan
Lywodraeth Cynulliad Cymru
Sponsored by
Welsh Assembly Government

Sgiliau Sylfaenol Cymru
Basic Skills

Loose

Connections

Rachel Trezise

ACCENT PRESS LTD

Chapter One
Third Time Lucky

It was 9.47 and from the window Rosemary could see the postman was delivering an oddly shaped parcel to the teenager in the semi across the road. It was round and wrapped in brown paper. It looked like a motorcycle helmet. Her repairman was seventeen minutes late. I'll make another coffee, Rosemary thought. I'll make another coffee and then I'll ring them, *again*.

She was about to move away from the window when she saw the white van pulling slowly into the cul-de-sac, the company's familiar purple and red emblem pasted on the side. She bunched the curtain in her fist, waiting for the worker to step out of the cab. Whole minutes slipped by, the van sitting motionless in the road, one wheel wedged against the kerb. Rosemary's fingers gripped the fabric until it turned wet in her hand.

When the van began to shake she let the curtain go. It fell back into position, an ugly crease left where her hand had been. The cab door opened, the hinges squeaking. Rosemary stood behind the gauzy curtain watching the figure emerge, her eyes narrowing. The repairman slammed the door and walked to the back of the vehicle. It *was* a man. Rosemary realised on seeing him that she'd hoped they'd send a woman this time. Women had a reputation for getting things done. The repairman looked a bit like an elf. He was short, and much too thin, with long, mousey hair tied into a messy ponytail. But even from behind the curtain she could see that his hands were quite beautiful. His fingers were slender and feminine, what her mother would have called *piano fingers*. As he unlocked the back doors she saw a winter sunbeam bounce off his gold signet ring.

This was the third repairman Rosemary's Internet Service Provider had sent in as many weeks. Rosemary was a translator and she worked from home. Most of her work involved legal documents. Her Internet connection had expired without explanation when she'd been about to complete a particularly important assignment. It was a purchase contract for a Corsican villa. Her failure to deliver the translated document to the French estate agency was delaying the entire sale. Her

2

commission fee was falling by the day. There were just a few details she needed to verify on the National Association of Estate Agents website, before e-mailing the contract to Paris. She could have used the computer suite at the central library, or popped next door to borrow Linda's laptop, but she refused to drive into the city centre, pay a small fortune to park, and then cart all of her paperwork and books through the arcade. Nor was she going to make a nuisance of herself by bothering her neighbours, not when she was paying hard-earned money for her own Internet connection. It was a matter of principle! And when the company had actually managed to fix the problem she was going to sue them for loss of earnings.

The first person they had sent was an obese man in his late thirties. Rosemary swore he had not showered in a month. He smelled like rotting vegetables. He sat at the PC and turned it on and off a couple of times. Rosemary had to leave the room because his smell was so bad. After half an hour he'd called her back into her little office under the stairs. 'A bit of a puzzle, this one, love,' he said.

Rosemary hated it when strangers called her 'love'. She leaned in the doorway, her hand covering her nose. He waved at the socket near the floor. 'Is this the main telephone line?' he said.

Rosemary nodded.

'Hmm, no chance of a cuppa is there then, love?' he said. 'I think I'll be here a while.'

She took four of her home-made banana flapjacks from the cooling tray on the counter and laid them on a saucer. She put them down on the desk with the tea. She wanted the job done quickly, and the best way to a fat man's heart was through his fat stomach. An hour or so later she could hear him packing his tools up. She put her novel down on the coffee table and ran into the office. 'Is it fixed?'

The repairman shook his head. 'They'll have to send someone else. I'm not up to date on all this IT business. I'm more of a phone-line man, me. I think the problem is with the computer itself. Computers! I'm not sure which way is up.' He laughed, his face turning red. His wide smile revealed a gap where one of his front teeth should have been. There were biscuit crumbs jammed in the corners of his mouth.

Rosemary didn't laugh.

The repairman shrugged. 'Well, don't worry about it too much, love,' he said. 'They'll send one of the young 'uns out first thing in the morning.'

She had to turn the air freshener to maximum when he left the house.

The second man had turned up a week later, a muscular twenty-something, wearing multi-coloured trainers, an iPod tucked into the breast pocket of his navy overall. He didn't seem much older than her sixteen-year-old son. 'All right?' he said briskly, marching into the house.

Rosemary followed him down the narrow hall. 'Just there,' she said pointing at the office door. The computer was already on. Every morning she checked the connection, hoping the glitch had mysteriously fixed itself overnight.

The repairman leaned over the desk and double-clicked the mouse, quickly opening and closing windows and browsers Rosemary had never seen before. 'The computer's fine,' he said. 'The report says the phone line is fine. It must be outside.' He went out into the street and held a small metal device against the telegraph post for a few minutes, and then dawdled back to the house, the device limp in his hand. He stood in front of the doorstep, not quite making eye contact with Rosemary. 'The post is dead,' he said. 'I can't understand it. The whole street must be out.' He sighed. 'They'll have to send someone else. It's not something I can deal with.'

'Why not?' Rosemary said.

'Health and safety.' He gestured at the telegraph pole. 'You'd need a cherry picker to look in there. I'm not qualified.' He was already swaggering down the drive. Had he been within arm's length, Rosemary might have slapped his stupid, juvenile face.

Now the new repairman was knocking on the front door. Rosemary took a deep breath and wiped her palms on the thighs of her jeans. She went into the hallway and saw the dark shadow of the petite figure through the frosted glass. She cleared her throat as she opened the door.

'Hi,' the man said. He had eyes the colour of honey, a deep, gooey yellow. Rosemary had never seen eyes that colour before. 'There's a problem with your Internet connection?' he said.

She stood aside to let him in, leading him down the hall and into the office. 'It's been broken for three weeks now,' she said, voice sharp, like an axe splitting wood. 'You're the *third* person they've sent.'

'Third time lucky, eh?' he said.

Rosemary turned the PC on. She pulled her leather computer chair out for him to sit down.

'They're nice,' he said. 'Is that you?' He was looking at the black and white photographs hanging from the picture rail. They'd been taken during summers at her grandparents' house. There was one for every year of her life, up until the age of fourteen when her parents had divorced, and her mother couldn't afford to spend summers in France any more. He was staring at the last in the series: Rosemary sitting on a stone bench in the courtyard, wearing a short puffball skirt, with Bébé, her grandfather's black cat, cradled in her gangly arms. 'It's not Britain, is it?' he said. He took a pair of spectacles out of his pocket and put them on, staring harder at the faded picture.

'Toulouse,' Rosemary said, surprised by his curiosity. Nobody looked at those photos any more. The kids had no interest in their heritage. 'My mother was French.'

'The pink city,' the man said, nodding knowingly. He sat in her leather chair but he didn't look at the monitor. 'Do you speak French?' He crossed his legs, the angular contour of his knee bone clear through the black cotton of his trousers.

'I'm a translator,' Rosemary said. 'That's what I do for a living. I work from home.' She wondered why she was telling him this. She paused. 'I need the Internet.'

'Say something,' he said. He was looking at her face. 'Say something in French.'

Rosemary's hands dropped from her hips. She knocked her arms against her sides like a little girl. '*Repare-moi cette putain de connection Internet*,' she said, a sentence that roughly translated to, 'Fix my bloody Internet.'

He understood the sarcasm, if not the language. 'OK,' he said, a broad smile splashed across his face. He turned to the screen. 'What's the problem exactly?' His smile evaporated, his ripe lower lip curved over its own little shadow.

Rosemary felt the severe tension that she'd forgotten for a moment seizing her nerves again. She folded her arms across her waist. 'The last guy they sent said the whole street was out. I know it's a lie because I saw the kid across the road take a parcel this morning. It came from eBay, I know it did, and that means he's using the Internet.' Her voice was bitter again. 'You know I'm going to sue when this is over?' she said. 'For loss of earnings and all of my expenses. I'm losing money every day.'

8

'That's a good idea,' the repairman said. He tapped at the keypad, his fingers dancing madly. Rosemary tried not to look at them. 'I'll leave you to it, shall I?' she said, turning out of the room.

'We get paid commission on call-outs,' the man said without looking up at her. Rosemary watched him work for a few seconds, waiting for his next sentence. The signet ring was on his right index finger. The seal was some kind of Celtic cross. There was no wedding ring but the skin on his ring finger was soft from having worn one at some time.

'What does that mean?' Rosemary said, remembering herself.

The repairman knelt down on the floor and studied the back of the tower, his bony limbs reminding her of a stick insect. 'It means that if there were people who were less than honest working for your ISP, they might tell you they weren't sure of the solution so they could earn themselves a few extra quid.' He waved a miniature screwdriver in the air. 'Then, if the job needs a second call-out, it means their mate can make some money too.'

'Is that what you're doing to me?'

'No!' He looked up at her, his strange yellow eyes glowing. 'Why would I tell you if that's what I was doing? You'd report me, wouldn't you?' He smiled.

Rosemary smiled back but she didn't know why. She was irked by the vague statement. There was something distasteful about it. She was annoyed by his calm manner and the interest he'd paid to her pictures. She wanted her Internet fixed. She wanted to check her e-mails. She took one last look at his pretty fingers. 'I'll just get you some tea,' she said, closing the door behind her.

'Thank you,' the repairman said as the woman disappeared from the room. He remembered that one of his colleagues, Big Mike, had said something about her tea. He'd said something about biscuits as well, that she made them herself, or said she did. The general view at the base was that there was a cable loose in the socket. He located the socket, knelt in front of it and inspected it, testing the cover with his thumb. They were right. One of the screws needed tightening. It was a five-second job but instead of doing it he sat back in the leather chair. He looked at the teenage girl in the photograph, sitting in a courtyard in France, her long, blonde hair curled and blowing in a light breeze. There was something striking

10

about her face. There still was. The woman was round at the edges now but her eyes hadn't lost any of their teenage intensity.

He wasn't sure why he'd felt the need to mention the scam. He'd never before breathed a word of it to a customer. He supposed he thought that admitting it cleared him somehow, that the woman would think he was trustworthy, friendly; that the others were the dishonest ones. That was roughly true in any case. Everyone at the company had been at it since before he'd started the job. Between them they'd discovered that they could dupe the vulnerable customers, lone females and pensioners, for two call-outs, but then the customers became impatient. They complained, and in turn the customer services department got suspicious. The scam wasn't something he particularly enjoyed but he was powerless to stop it, on his own. He was the last link in the chain this time. Often they sent him last because people tended to trust him. He quite liked this woman though. He felt uncomfortable lying to her. He'd drink his tea, give it an hour, and distract her with chit-chat about France.

Chapter Two
Abduction

Rosemary stomped into the kitchen and stood at the worktop. She pushed the plastic lever on the electric kettle, the way she always did when she found herself with guests in her house. It was a reflex action. But she didn't take the teacup out of the cupboard. She didn't take the spoon from the cutlery tray. She didn't pull the top from the vintage sugar canister. She stared out of the window and listened to the kettle boiling, the water bubbling. She was still hot with irritation, a thin layer of sweat bleeding from her hairline. The con that the repairman had hinted at sounded possible. It would explain why there was no sure explanation for the fault.

On the decking outside, a she-cat was eating a discarded chunk of cooked chicken, her sex clear from a loosely fitting pink collar. Another cat was trying to get at the chicken, but each time it made a bid for the meat the she-cat snarled, her teeth milk-white and sharp as needles. After a few attempts, the she-cat pounced, catching the thin skin of the other cat's ear with her outstretched claw. It yelped and skulked backwards four paces before fleeing over the garden wall. As it did, an idea entered Rosemary's head, as clear and flawless as if God himself had put it there. 'I'll kidnap the repairman,' she said to herself. She had never heard her voice sound so pure and determined, as though the air in the kitchen had become a microphone. It was as if she had discovered a cure for cancer and she was announcing her brainchild to the world. 'He's a small guy,' she said, reasoning with herself, 'smaller than me. I'll hold him hostage until he's fixed it.'

There was a cream vanity case hidden under the bed frame in her room. She kneeled on the floor and pulled it out. The creases in the discoloured leather were filled with thick wisps of dust. She pressed the nickel button with her thumb and the buckle popped open with a soft ping. Inside, she found old bottles of massage oils, and a half-used tube of KY Jelly, its top glued to its body. There were unopened packets of condoms, flavoured, ribbed, Fetherlite. The white use-by dates stamped on the packaging were years old. Remnants from a past life. She couldn't remember the last time she'd had sexual intercourse. She was only thirty-seven. Apparently that was the age when a woman hit her sexual prime. But sex had been a chore since she'd had her daughter fourteen years ago.

At first she and her husband had tried to schedule it in. They sent the kids to their grandparents. They lit tea lights. They ate shellfish and asparagus, strawberries and watermelon. They smothered one another's bodies with edible chocolate-flavoured paint. But she worried about her stretch marks. She made him turn the lights out. She began to fall asleep in the middle of foreplay. Like a magician turning silk handkerchiefs into white rabbits, sexual chemistry vanished as soon as true biology reared its head.

She pushed her hand deeper into the case until her fingers touched cold metal. She pulled the handcuffs out and they smelt rusty, like old coins. They were something she'd won at an Ann Summers party in Linda's house four years ago, along with a cheap bottle of red wine. She'd drunk the wine that very night, but the handcuffs had never been used. She carried them with her arm outstretched, the way someone might carry a recovered weapon, a knife or a gun. The frames of the cuffs were decorated with bands of black ostrich feathers. She crept downstairs, missing the second-last step because she knew it creaked. She stood outside the office for a moment, listening to the silence from within. She hid the handcuffs behind her back. She opened the door.

The repairman was sitting in her chair, staring at the pictures. 'You know there's something about that image,' he said. 'I can't take my eyes off it.'

'Really?' Rosemary stood behind him. She rested her elbow on the back of the chair, leaning down next to him to share his point of view. His hair smelt of medicated shampoo. 'Why not?' she said. The repairman kept looking at the photograph, his mouth open. 'I don't know,' he said, his voice a whisper. 'It's something about your eyes. They look sad, and happy at the same time.'

Rosemary reached for his hand. It was cold and almost lifeless. She looked at it for a moment, positioned in her own hand, before pulling it gently behind the chair. He wasn't going to fight. She couldn't believe it. She couldn't believe what she was doing. Swiftly she secured the cuff around his wrist, as tight as it would go. His hand jerked as he resisted but Rosemary was too quick. She slipped the other

'How am I meant to do that?' the man said. He yanked his arm towards the keyboard and the metal cuff grazed the soft black leather again. 'I'm right-handed. I can't do anything with these stupid things on me. Get the key.'

Rosemary was stumped. She hadn't thought about this. She was silent until the man said, 'You know, you're not the first female client who's tried to come on to me like this. Once, on the council estate in Ely, a girl put a pornographic video on. I didn't know what to do. I didn't encourage it. I was kneeling down on the floor trying to fix her phone socket.' There was an impish grin playing on his face. 'All she had to do was ask me for my number.'

'Why the hell would I come on to *you*?' Rosemary said. 'I'm a married woman with two teenage children.' As the words hit the air they sounded unfamiliar. She *was* a married woman with two teenage children, and she must have used that sentence a hundred thousand times. But now it sounded like a lie. Her husband was at work. He was a partner in an accounting firm in St Mellons. These days he was in work even when he wasn't in work. He'd come in around seven in the evening and sit at the dining table poring over other people's tax returns. When he wasn't there he was at his mother's house.

18

She was seventy-five and suffering from moderate dementia. Often she mistook her son for her late husband and she'd ring their house in the middle of the night, demanding he leave his whore of a fancy woman and go back to his long-suffering wife.

He refused to put her into a care home. He'd suggested once that she come to live with them and Rosemary refused outright. She was the one who worked from home. She was the one who would become primary carer, attending to her mother-in-law's whims, emptying her commode. She and her mother-in-law had never got on. When they'd first met she'd called Rosemary a 'mumper', a West Country description for a gypsy. And now Rosemary suspected that she was exaggerating her symptoms, causing trouble for the sake of it, because that was the kind of woman her mother-in-law was. She demanded attention every minute of the day. She'd worn a white dress on the day of her only son's wedding, for Christ's sake.

Rosemary and her husband barely spoke any more. It was as if they lived in a house that was haunted by the ghosts of themselves. They'd become one of those couples who sat at the table of a restaurant reading the menu over and over, staring out of the window, or at the other customers, wondering what to say to one another. They'd become the sort of people they used to laugh at when they were in their early twenties, when it was just them against the rest of the world.

She didn't feel much like a mother any more, either. Daniel was sixteen. He already had a girlfriend. Her parents let him stay at their house in Llandaff on weekends. 'In the guestroom, right?' Rosemary had said when she'd found out. For a few months he'd hidden it, claiming to have been staying at Jason's, his friend from English class. 'No, Mom,' he'd said, talking in an American accent that had made her cringe. 'In her room, duh. She's got an en-suite as well.' When Rosemary had tried to talk to him about contraception he said his girlfriend had been on the pill since she was thirteen. He said they'd already slept together in a tent at a music festival the previous summer. Rosemary had slapped him hard across the face, something she was ashamed of now. She'd always planned to be a liberal parent, someone her children could talk to, no matter what. 'I was only joking,' he'd said, holding his hand over his jaw. 'As if I'd tell *you* anyway. We've got sex counsellors at school for that.'

Rosemary's daughter, Chantelle, was fourteen. She was a child trapped in the body of a fully formed woman. Her breasts were already bigger than Rosemary's would ever be, but she was still determined to get an enlargement as soon as she was old enough. It was a subject on which they could find no compromise. Rosemary was strongly opposed to plastic surgery. She'd tried to teach her children that all human beings were beautiful in their own way. She couldn't understand how she'd managed to raise a daughter whose only goal was to bare her fake breasts in a tabloid newspaper.

No matter how hard you tried, outside influences always thwarted your attempts to control your own life. Sooner or later, you turned into your own parents. The tracks stretched out before her were the ones her mother had left behind. Everything that she had hated about her mother had become characteristics in herself: her anxiousness, her impatience, her bad temper. She giggled at the irony of it. 'Time turns us all into cantankerous old bats,' she said quietly, thinking aloud.

Chapter Three
Women

A few silent minutes passed and the repairman looked irritated, his eyes cast down to the floor. He was holding his head in his willowy, free hand, his clean, half-moon fingernails pressed on his temple. Rosemary kicked him again, the toe of her pump tapping his knee bone. 'Do you prefer fake breasts, or real ones?' she said.

He looked up at her, eyes impatient. 'What?' he said.

'Come on, fake tits or real ones? Surely the thing that's attractive about the female breast is the fact that they're a source of nourishment for newborn babies. Who in the world would find two lumps of plastic appealing? Those girls in the magazines look like freaks. If you stuck a pin in their cleavage you'd expect them to burst like a pair of balloons.'

'I'm not sure I'd know the difference,' the man said.

Rosemary frowned. 'Of course you'd know the difference. Fake breasts don't move. You lie down, they stay sticking up. They stay there forever. When the woman has died and the body has decomposed, they're still there.' Just two sacks of jelly left buried in the ground, she thought. In millions of years, when explorers were raking through our remains, that's all they'd find, bags and bags of white silicone caked in brown earth. They'd wonder what the hell we'd been doing with our lives.

The repairman looked thoughtful. 'Did you ever hear about that murder case,' he said, 'where they found a prostitute chopped up and stuffed into bin bags? Her body was so badly mutilated, her dental records were useless. But her implants had serial numbers. They used them to identify her.'

'How are they going to identify you?' Rosemary said.

The repairman flinched, the chain between the handcuffs rattling.

'Sorry,' she said. 'Bad joke.' Changing tack, she said, 'What about vaginal surgery? Some women have that, you know. I've seen programmes about it. Mothers and daughters going to the clinic together to get their labia trimmed as if it's some sort of normal activity, as if they're off to have their legs waxed. Do you know how ridiculous that is?'

The repairman shook his head. 'They'll look

for me,' he said. 'They know where I am.' His eyes were dark, the yellow irises turning green.

'I blame pornography,' Rosemary said. 'Women today think that they're sexually free, so they watch porn, like your customer in Ely. Then they get this idea in their heads that there's such a thing as a perfect vagina, and then they want one. They're paying money to have parts of their genitals hacked off while human rights groups in Africa are working overtime to ban female genital mutilation. That's how ridiculous it is! We're not evolving, we're going backwards.'

'It's not my fault,' the man said.

'I know,' Rosemary said. While she'd been talking she'd thought of a way to improve the situation. She could fix the connection with directions from the repairman. It couldn't be that difficult, could it? 'By the way,' she said, 'you can leave any time you like, all you've got to do is fix the Internet connection and you can be on your way. I know that you're sort of physically challenged at the moment but I'm not useless am I? Just tell me what to do, and I'll do it. You can direct me.'

The repairman was silent, so she went back to her rant. 'The other thing about pornography,' she said, 'is that it dictates the sort of sex people should be having. Just the other day I was flicking through one of my daughter's magazines. Know what I found?'

The repairman was staring at his bony knees.

'A guide on how to perform fellatio,' Rosemary said. 'Not your average run-of-the-mill sort of fellatio though. The kind where you take the man's member right down into your throat. That's the way men like it, apparently. The journalist who wrote it was a woman. She reckoned there's a knack to switching your gag reflex off. With a little practice you can teach yourself how not to vomit on your boyfriend's penis! My daughter's fourteen years old.'

'I didn't write it!' the repairman said, voice sharp.

'I know you didn't write it!' Rosemary said, annoyed. 'I told you, a woman wrote it.' She'd thought about writing a letter of complaint to the editor but knew it was a waste of time. They filled those kinds of magazines with sex on purpose. Sex sold, especially to teenagers, who were so curious about it. She wished now that she'd never found it. She wished she'd never been in her daughter's room, going through her private things. She'd found her diary and skimmed the first three or four pages, another deed she was now deeply ashamed of. It was something she'd never forgiven her own mother for, until now. Standing there, surrounded by posters of near-naked men, with that wealth of secret knowledge in her hand, the diary's blue cover plastered with love-heart stickers and band names, she just wasn't able to resist.

She hadn't been looking for anything in particular, and she hadn't found it either. There wasn't any writing, only blue biro doodles of gargantuan breasts, like bulbous figures of eights, lying on their sides, bold dots dabbed in the middle to represent nipples. Had she been working, she wouldn't have gone near the room. She hated the awful smell of patchouli oil that Chantelle insisted on pouring on to her bedclothes. There wasn't a laundry detergent strong enough to get rid of it. Instead, the oil contaminated the other items in the cycle. If she didn't spend a good fifteen minutes separating the family's linen before a wash, the whole house smelled of it. She wondered now if there was a film or a play that she could take her daughter to see, something that would educate her about the diverse nature of breasts.

'Have you ever seen *The Vagina Monologues*?' she said.

The repairman rubbed the side of his face against his shoulder, like a sheep trying to scratch itself on a fence post. 'Please,' he said, mortified. 'Stop talking about breasts and va, vag–' He couldn't say the word. 'Women's parts,' he said finally. 'I'm not sexist, all right? I'm all for equality. If it's any comfort, I ran away when I saw what that woman was watching.'

'Did you?' Rosemary said.

'Yes.'

'But you can't run away now, can you?' she said. 'You're handcuffed to the chair.' She noticed the name tag on his overall pocket for the first time, the letters punched into the plastic. Aaron, it said. 'You're in my house now, Aaron,' Rosemary said. 'I'll talk about whatever I like.'

The repairman sat up, about to say something. His full lips formed around a new word, but then he closed his mouth and slumped back into the chair.

'There's no such thing as equality, Aaron,' Rosemary said. 'So what if women become plumbers? So what if you have to call a manhole cover a person-hole cover? That doesn't mean jack shit. Women still aren't paid the same wage.' She pushed a bulky French-language dictionary out of her way and sat back against the wall, pulling her legs up on to the edge of the desk. 'I've got a theory,' she said. 'I think the suffragettes got it wrong. I think the bra-burners did more harm than good. We should never have started work. Now we *have* to work, because you need more than one wage to run a household. People look down on you if you *don't* work. If you live on your husband's income, people call you a gold-digger, a scrounger. Or they think that you're a bimbo, too brainless to carve out your own career. So fine! We go to work. We work the same hours as our husbands. We put up with all of the same workplace pressures. Somewhere along the line we give up a promotion or two in favour of taking maternity leave to bear a couple of kids. Men can't have babies yet, can they? Doesn't stop them wanting them, though.'

'I don't want kids,' Aaron said.

Rosemary ignored him. 'So now we're working. Now we've got spending power, choices. We can buy a pair of shoes without asking our husband's permission. So we're equal, right? Wrong! Who does the cooking and the cleaning? Women. They spend all day in the office and then they come home and cook the food. Not any sort of food. Oh no! It's got to be home-made, hand-cooked from scratch. Every time they turn the TV on, there's Nigella bloody Lawson stirring coconut milk into a beef and aubergine curry. Cooking is sexy. Baking is cool. Feeding your family on fresh, organic ingredients is the least you should do. Don't even think about taking the kids to McDonald's or dropping a handful of frozen chips into the deep fat fryer. You do that and Jamie Oliver will be on the doorstep with the food police, quicker than you can say *Turkey flippin' twizzler*!'

Rosemary wrung her hands. 'Look at you,' she said. 'You can fix a computer, you can hold a screwdriver. What's so difficult about the "on" button on a washing machine? I know exactly how many steps it takes to get from the washing machine to the washing line. Ten. I know it by heart. My husband doesn't even know where the pegs are kept.'

'A woman's work is never done,' the repairman said.

Rosemary huffed. 'You're telling me,' she said.

'Listen.' The repairman sat up in the chair, his free arm balanced on the leather arm. He was trying to look confident, but he just looked absurd. The black ostrich feathers had caused some sort of reaction. There was a pink patch on the skin on the back of his hand. 'You're clearly stressed. Don't take this the wrong way, but your doctor could help you out with that, give you something to relax. Or you could go on holiday. When was the last time you went on holiday?'

'How can I afford a holiday?' Rosemary said. 'I can't afford a weekend in a tent until I get my assignment e-mailed. And I can't do that without a working Internet connection, can I?' She looked up at him. 'When was the last time you went on holiday?'

'The summer,' he said. 'Prague.'

'Nice,' Rosemary said. 'I hope you enjoyed yourself. Might be the last holiday you get for a while.'

Aaron sneaked a glance at the wall clock above the desk. If it was right it was almost eleven o'clock, the short hand pointing at the elegant XI Roman numeral. He'd been here for just over an hour and he'd made sixty quid but he wasn't sure how long he could keep up the act. He couldn't take any more talk about pornography or body parts. But if he could keep a dialogue going, he could stretch it to a hundred and twenty minutes.

'You know you'll have to let me go at some point,' he said. 'I don't know what's wrong with your connection and I can't figure out the problem while I'm handcuffed to this chair.' He yanked at the chain between the cuffs, testing the strength of the metal. He wouldn't be able to break out, but he expected her to hand the key over when she'd got whatever was troubling her off her chest.

He was sure he wasn't in any immediate danger. He could feel the weight of his mobile phone in his shirt pocket. He'd be able to reach it in a second flat. 'What's going to happen when your husband gets home from work?' he said. For some reason he'd never imagined that she was married. Divorced, perhaps, but his colleagues had never mentioned there being a man in the house. Usually, when there was a man in the house, trivial faults like loose wires were checked before a request for a call-out was made. 'Or when your children get back from school?' he added, trying to keep the momentum up. The woman's eyes were glazed. She didn't seem to be listening. 'I'm sure there would be jail time for kidnapping.'

'What do I care?' she said, frowning down

into her lap. 'That would be a holiday, wouldn't it? Someone could feed me for a change. The taxpayer could take care of the rent. I could do classes, woodwork, creative writing.' Her voice was composed, her tone level. She didn't seem to think that she was doing anything wrong. For the first time in a whole hour, Aaron felt a trace of fear deep down in his belly. He glanced around again for a window, knowing there wasn't one. He missed daylight, and the heating was on full. He was sweating. 'Listen,' he said.

The woman looked up from her manicured fingernails.

'What's the real problem here?' It seemed obvious that there was more to all of this than a broken Internet connection.

Chapter Four
The Truth

'What do you mean?' Rosemary said.

She was suddenly alert, sitting up on the desk, her arms clutched around her knees. She wondered if he knew something. Perhaps her Internet Service Provider had kept all of her movements on record. They could intercept e-mails. That's how criminals got caught. She believed 'cookies' was the correct term for the tracking devices stored on a computer's hard disk. It was a fitting name.

She should have been aware of this. She could often detect that Chantelle had been into her office, looking at plastic surgery clinics online. She could type 'land' into a search engine and the address of the Landauer Cosmetic Surgery Group would pop up. Once she'd seen a computer programme advertised on an American infomercial on cable TV. The presenter claimed it could make a copy of text typed on any given keyboard. They were aiming it at bored and mistrustful housewives who suspected their hubbies of looking at porn.

No! She was being paranoid. She was always being paranoid. Internet Service Providers couldn't give away any personal information unless it was part of an ongoing criminal investigation. She giggled, her throat dry and tight, her conscience pressing down on her like a vice. She wished she could cut it out of herself like a tumour. She wasn't doing anything wrong. Not really. She hadn't broken any laws. She hadn't broken any commandments. 'What do you mean?' she said, repeating herself. 'Don't be an amateur psychologist, just be a good repairman. This is about my broken Internet connection. I need it to be fixed.'

'Why?' Aaron said. It was clear now that there was something wrong. She was avoiding eye contact, picking at pieces of lint on the thighs of her trousers.

'I told you why,' she said. 'I've got a purchase contract here for a French villa. It needs to be translated into English and sent to an estate agent in Paris.' She waved a purple folder in the air. 'Until it gets there I don't get paid. Three weeks it's been here. I need the Internet. I need it to check over a few of the finer points. Why am I even explaining this to you? It's none of your business. Just fix the damn thing. That's your job.' She slapped the folder down on the desk, a pen rolling off the edge.

'I'll do it if you let me go,' Aaron said. This situation was ridiculous. The woman was impossible.

'No you won't,' Rosemary shouted. 'You won't fix it. You'll say you don't know what the problem is. You'll apologise and then you'll leave and then I'll have to wait for someone else.'

'What else do you need the Internet for?' Aaron said. He meant the question to sound caring but he was shouting now too, almost against his own will. The woman was holding her head in her hands, her palms blocking her eyes. Her feet were trembling. Aaron knew he was on to something. He took a deep breath. 'What do you *really* need the Internet for?' he said.

'I told you!' she said, voice desperate. Her throat was clogged, the words filled with mucus.

'No,' Aaron said. 'If you needed the money you'd put the file on to a disk. You'd take it to an Internet café in town. It's not about an Internet connection. It's about *this* Internet connection. It's something to do with this computer.' He waved his free hand at the monitor.

As he did the woman moved slightly, starting the screensaver. A slideshow of French landmarks glided slowly across the screen: the Arc de Triomphe, the Champs-Elysées, Montmartre, the Eiffel Tower, various figures of imposing, grey stone. The woman was crying, not sobbing, just crying, water pouring in thin streams down her hands.

'What is it?' he said.

'OK,' she said, spitting. She opened her hands and showed her face. Her skin was pink and wet. Some of her black make-up was smudged across the top of her cheekbone. 'I'm having an affair,' she said.

There! Rosemary had said it. Those four words had been balancing on the tip of her tongue for twelve months. She was always afraid that they would jump out over dinner, or during sleep. She worried that she'd voice them by accident like someone suffering from Tourette's syndrome. She thought she'd feel embarrassed telling a stranger her great secret, but her relief outweighed the shame. She let her shoulders drop. She wiped a tear away from her eye with the cuff of her sweater. 'Say something then,' she said.

The repairman was staring at the computer. She was expecting him to criticise her, to call her a hypocrite. Maybe part of her wanted that, like a Catholic at confession craving Hail Marys. When she was punished she could repent. He shook his head, looking amused. He grinned. 'I don't understand,' he said. 'You're having an affair.' He shrugged. 'What has that got to do with me?'

Rosemary realised that the repairman had no interest in her personal life. He wasn't her husband. He wasn't a priest. He had no power over her. She looked at the keyboard on the desk between them, the dust and dried flakes of pink nail polish trapped in the ridges between the buttons. She thought about all the mischievous words she had created with its keys. She remembered the X that she'd used too easily, making cyber-kisses run across the white screen. 'Don't you get it?' she said. 'An Internet affair. He lives in Bordeaux. We talk to each other by e-mail.'

Aaron's eyes flashed with understanding. 'Ah,' he said.

Rosemary had met André on a social networking site the previous November. He had found her. He had asked her to be his 'friend'. He was older than her, in his early fifties. His profile photo looked like a tired version of God. A large man with tame, brown eyes, a mane of wild white hair, and a long white beard streaked with thin slivers of grey. He was an art teacher in a high school. Rosemary accepted his request and then sent him a message in French, asking why he was interested in her. She'd never met him. They shared no mutual friends. She had no relatives in the Bordeaux area. In fact, she'd never come across his surname before, but she looked it up: *Arceneaux*, a common, occupational title meaning maker or seller of guns. Less than twenty-four hours later his bold reply arrived in her inbox. 'Because you're a beautiful woman, of course.'

The response made her study her own profile picture. It had been taken on a family drive to Barry Island. She was sitting on a bench on the Victorian walkway above the beach, the palm tree behind her hiding the true nature of the Welsh climate. She was looking away from the camera, smiling at a bird on the ground. Nothing in the photo struck her as particularly attractive, but for a thirty-seven-year-old she supposed she had quite good skin.

When she looked very closely at the photograph she could see the toe of one of Daniel's trainers in the background. She remembered that he had spoiled the whole day by letting everyone know that Fred West's ashes had been scattered into the Barry Island sea.

'Don't be so stupid,' his father had said. 'Why would they scatter the ashes of a Gloucestershire serial killer here?'

Daniel boosted his argument with information about how, as a child in the 1950s, Fred West was regularly taken on day trips to Barry Island. When he grew up and became a serial killer he continued the family tradition by taking his wife and their kids to the Welsh beach. 'You can find pictures of him in Barry Island in any number of True Crime books,' he'd said, voice firm. Chantelle, who had wanted to go to the Cardiff Bay retail park anyway, stuck her fingers into her throat, pretending to gag.

So, Rosemary had written back to André, using his own cheeky, brief style. She wrote one sentence that said, 'Don't be so silly, I'm average at best.' She could see now that it had been a blatant fish for another compliment. She wanted confirmation, certainty. Nobody had described her as beautiful for decades. Not that she could remember, anyway. Her husband's voice had become a sound that she didn't hear any more. It existed in the background, like the tumble dryer in the utility room, or the distant traffic on the M4. White noise. If he'd said it, she hadn't noticed.

A day later, André came back with another lone sentence that said, 'Trust me, I'm an artist, I've got a brilliant eye.' At the time it was midwinter and her husband was busy collecting clients' data for the tax deadline in the New Year. There wasn't much translation work around. She spent her days honing her skills by e-mailing André, who spoke no English at all. Of course, she'd learned a long time ago, back in her schooldays, that a woman should never trust a man who made a point of implying that he was trustworthy. But in cyberspace those rules didn't seem to apply. It wasn't as if they were going out on dates.

André made Rosemary laugh, for the first time in many years. He sent her a cartoon strip that he had drawn. In it, Rosemary was dressed in Wonder Woman's blue, star-speckled hot pants and calf-length red boots. She was standing at the top of the Empire State Building throwing spears at saucer-shaped UFOs. He'd managed to portray her whole face with four ticks of a felt tip.

Other times he told her stories about artists, how Picasso's first word was 'lápiz', the Spanish word for pencil, or how Degas despised the colour yellow. He told her how Dalí's *The Persistence of Memory* had been inspired by staring at a runny piece of Camembert cheese on a hot August day, how Botticelli suffered from unrequited love for a married noblewoman called Simonetta Vespucci, his subject in *The Birth of Venus*, and how he was buried at her feet in a churchyard in Florence.

Rosemary was sucked into his stories like a bobble of fluff in the path of a vacuum cleaner. He talked so passionately about his job, it was impossible not to be. Conversation was a forgotten art in her house. Nobody really talked about anything. They just plodded through the day like zombies on the trail of human flesh. She'd realised this after only a week of mailing with André. And one night, at the dining table, she'd tested her family, making sure she wasn't mistaken.

'Tell me what you like about G-Unit,' she'd said to Daniel as he poured a glass of Coke. He frowned at her for a few moments as if she'd been talking in French rather than about his favourite hip-hop band. Then he took a gulp of his drink. 'They're cool, init?' he said, before belching. When the kids had been excused, her husband opened up his case on the table. He took his calculator out and tapped at the keys. Then he noted a figure down with a biro. 'Talk to me about something,' Rosemary said, having filled and closed the dishwasher.

'Like what?' he said.

'I don't know.' She shrugged. 'Anything. How was your day?'

'I won't bore you with the details,' he said, turning back to his work.

Somewhere between Christmas and New Year Rosemary had found herself standing in an empty room in the National Museum, staring at Cézanne's *Still Life with Apples and Teapot*. The orange scarf Chantelle had bought for her from Marks & Spencer's was pulled up over her mouth. A few days earlier André had sent an e-mail entitled 'Seven Questions to Ask Yourself When Looking at Art'. They were: Does the artwork tell a story? Are there any issues in the work? What kind of images, objects, materials or symbols are there? Does it have a title? Is colour important? Does the work interact with the space it is in? How was the work made? She had memorised all seven and she was applying them to a painting she'd never seen before, despite it being in her city since 1952. She wasn't a zombie. She was alive.

Chapter Five
The Truth Hurts

Over the course of a year, Rosemary had come to rely on André's e-mails, the way a kicked dog relies on a treat. For a few minutes each week, he beamed her up out of her routine, ordinary life and put her somewhere special. His stories about artists were like food for her soul. Getting an e-mail from him put her in such a good mood that she'd sing pop songs while doing the household chores. She put extra slices of beef into her husband's sandwiches and extra fabric conditioner into the family's wash. She'd bake batches of fairy cakes and carefully apply the coconut icing with a piping bag.

Not getting an e-mail produced the opposite effect. She'd stock her husband's lunch box with egg-mayo sandwich filler, spread on stale bread. She'd stay up late and sit in her office, an old typewriter pushed up against the door. She'd read and reread the last e-mail she'd received, drinking the words like wine, looking for secret codes in the text, like a hopeless Christian with a cheap Gideon's Bible.

Sometimes, before she fell asleep, she fantasised about running away to Bordeaux. She thought about sitting on a sunny terrace overlooking an emerald green vineyard, drinking a Cabernet Sauvignon, like a real-life Shirley Valentine. She fantasised about a dirty weekend with André. She would take the Eurostar and he would meet her at the station and take her overnight case. They'd hold hands and stare at the paintings in the Parisian galleries. They'd order room service and get crumbs from their croissants in the bed.

She fantasised about sitting for one of André's portraits. She'd lie naked on a red leather chaise longue, a flimsy white sheet covering her pubis, her body steeped in André's undivided attention. They were only fantasies; they were allowed to be clichés. She had no intention of carrying them out. Sometimes she only fantasised that she was a student in André's art class, listening to him talk about the way to create a realistic vanishing point.

Lately, though, his e-mails had become fewer and fewer. She was lucky if she got one a fortnight. Each one opened with an apology. 'Je suis désolé …' He said he was busy with marking, but he'd never been busy with marking before.

Also the e-mails' content was becoming shorter. Often they'd only contain one uninspired sentence. 'When the *Mona Lisa* was stolen from the Louvre a guard noticed it missing the morning it was taken but assumed that the museum photographer had taken it.' Or, 'Rubens's *Massacre of the Innocents* was actually painted by his students – he only added the finishing touches later.'

When she did get an e-mail she worried that it would be the last. She had nightmares about her inbox remaining forever empty. She'd get up in the night to check her mail and often when there was nothing, she felt suicidal. Please let there be *something*, she'd think, just an offer for half-price Viagra, or a cheap penis enlargement procedure in a Venezuelan clinic. Anything! Something! The last e-mail she'd got had been a few weeks before she lost her connection. As ever it had begun with an apology, which was followed by three empty lines. On the fourth, it said, 'Work, work, work. No play. More soon. AAx.'

The repairman sighed, blowing a stray hair out of his face. He was gazing at Rosemary, waiting for her to speak. 'Actually, it's not really an affair,' she said in an attempt to brush off the confession, 'more an ongoing conversation.' The repairman was silent. 'He talks to me about art,' Rosemary said. 'He's an art teacher, and an artist. He just talks to me about his work. It's quite fascinating. He lives in Bordeaux.'

'French,' the repairman said. 'Like you.'

'Yes, French,' Rosemary said, her voice sour. As if nationality had anything to do with it! She was beginning to regret telling the repairman anything. 'I've never met him,' she said, 'so it's not technically an affair. That was a Freudian slip.' She tried to smile, her shoulders hunched. 'Who could resist a Frenchman?'

'You ought to be careful who you talk to on the Internet,' Aaron said. 'It's a dangerous place. It's no different to going out alone at night. In some cases it's worse. When you can't see who you're talking to, how do you know they're genuine? There are thieves, hackers, not to mention the perverts. He could be just trying to get at your bank details, or your phone number, or your address.'

He nodded to confirm his point, his eyes serious. 'Only last week some fella in London was stabbed and mugged. He was responding to an advert for a car. He had the money to pay for it in a plastic grocery bag, five thousand pounds. There was no car, just a couple of wrong'uns armed with guns. They saw him coming.'

'Don't be so absurd,' Rosemary said. 'André's a real person. That's his real name. He's an art teacher at a school. How else would he know so much about art? He told me that when Picasso was born, the birth was so difficult, and the baby was so weak, the midwife thought he was stillborn. She put the baby down on a chair and turned to attend to the mother. Also he told me that Picasso was christened with twenty-three names but Picasso wasn't one of them. Picasso was his mother's middle name. His father's name was Blasco, or Basclo, something like that.' She wasn't managing to control her excitement very well.

'How do you know?' Aaron said.

'André!' Rosemary said. 'André told me.'

'I mean, how do you know that this André is a real person? How do you know that he lives in Bordeaux? How do you know he's not some psychotic stalker watching you from a house across the road?'

Rosemary laughed loudly, the sound echoing around the tiny room. 'Because I do,' she said. 'I just do.' She thought about his profile image. He was an old man, with lanky, white hair. If he was pretending to be someone else surely he'd use a better picture. He'd pretend to be young, dark, and athletic.

'He's never asked me for any personal details,' Rosemary said. Too bad, because she would have given them to him without question. She often wondered why he didn't try to further their relationship, why he didn't ask her for more pictures, why he didn't suggest a meeting. She supposed that somewhere in her subconscious she had decided that he was married with children, that his family had no interest in his career. Like her, he was unappreciated, undervalued. He was lonely. 'Nobody could know that much about art unless they really loved it,' Rosemary said. 'He's cultured and passionate, all the things British men aren't.' She looked at the wall behind Aaron's head, staring into the distance. 'He told me things that only an artist would know.'

'Do you love him?' Aaron blurted out, unexpectedly. The question was born from a mixture of jealousy and contempt. He thought that if the woman was going to the trouble of having an affair, it should have been with him. He was a real, physical person, sitting right there in front of her. He could talk to her about graphic design, and he could make sure her Internet connection was working.

But Aaron had never had any luck with women. His own wife had left him for another man after only six months of marriage. He'd been on his own for six years now and, though he didn't like to admit it, he'd been very lonely since his mother had died two years ago. 'Well, do you?' he said, prompting her. He had some leverage on her now. He could use the knowledge against her if the situation took a turn for the worse. Plus, another hour of heart-to-heart was another hundred pounds in the bank.

'Of course I don't love him!' Rosemary said. 'How can you love someone you've never met?' Love was an emotion that took over and changed the course of your life. It made you want to have children. It allowed you to make compromises. Love was what had turned her into what she was today – a bored housewife and mother of two.

It wasn't love. It was just some kind of infatuation. But if that was the case, why was she so frantic to hear from him again? Why did his lack of contact make her feel so awful? It was the danger, the excitement of seeing a foreign man's name in her inbox. It shone out of the small list of companies and work colleagues there, like a diamond in a heap of coal. It was the anticipation of what he was going to say next. For a whole year their unusual connection had remained pure *because* they had never met, because they had never even touched. It was the vulnerable nature of their relationship that turned her on. It wasn't safe. It wasn't reliable. It wasn't predictable. It was the opposite of what her marriage was. 'We're friends,' she said. 'Pen pals, that's all. I love the things he says, though. Does that help?'

Aaron frowned. 'Have you ever heard of the term, "grooming"?' he said.

'I told you,' Rosemary said. 'I've got a fourteen-year-old daughter.'

'There you go then,' Aaron shrugged.

'What on earth would André be grooming me for?' she said.

'I told you. Burglary! Rape! There's nothing to say an artist can't be a serial killer, is there? In fact, Hitler was an artist. Grown women go missing after meeting dodgy men on the

54

Internet all the time. It really isn't that difficult to fool someone, you know. What does he know about you? He knows that you speak French, so he talks to you in French. You're half French, so he tells you he lives in Bordeaux. You probably told him, somewhere along the line, that you like Picasso. Now he's an expert on Picasso. They tell you what they know you want to hear. People like you are too trusting.'

'It's none of your business anyway,' Rosemary said.

Aaron shook his head. He was frustrated now. 'I didn't ask to be here, did I?' he said. 'I could have had you up and running by now. If you hadn't handcuffed me to the chair I'd be gone. You could have been online, talking to lover boy, talking to Jean Pierre.'

'He's not a boy,' Rosemary said. 'He's not my lover, either.'

'You don't really know what he is, do you?' Aaron said. The metal cuff was beginning to bite at his wrist. The feathers were aggravating his skin. The clock said it was gone twelve. He already had more money than he knew what to do with. He wanted to go now. 'How about you unlock the cuffs?' he said. 'I'll fix the connection and there'll be no more said about it.'

Rosemary looked thoughtful. She slid off the edge of the desk and stood facing him, calmly considering his offer.

'What do you think?' he said, encouraging her. 'What happens in the French translator's office stays in the French translator's office.' He smiled.

The woman wiped at the dark make-up smudge on her cheekbone, spreading the stain further across her face. 'Do you know what?' she said. 'I forgot to bring you your tea.' She marched out of the room. Aaron bit his bottom lip.

Chapter Six
Torture

When Rosemary got back to the office five minutes later, she was holding a mug and a plate of Viennese Whirls. She put the biscuits down on the desk. 'How dare you insult my intelligence!' she shrieked. She was angry at the repairman's comment about her not knowing who André really was. She was angry because he was right. She'd been the first to mention Picasso. He'd asked her who her favourite artists were. She hadn't known much about art then. She'd said Picasso because there was an article about him in the newspaper on her desk. She glared at the repairman, her hand shaking. Tea splashed on to the laminate floor.

'How dare you call me stupid? I'm not stupid! I'm a grown woman. I'm a professional. I'm streetwise. I know what I'm doing.' She wasn't sure why those last two statements were necessary. She wasn't streetwise. She hadn't been into town for months. She had done all of her shopping online until her connection broke down. Now, she sent her husband to the

Tesco Express on his way home from work. She winced at the shock of daylight when she left the house to peg washing out. Her whole life revolved around the computer and she was sick of it. And she *clearly* didn't know what she was doing. She was obsessed with a man she'd never met, so obsessed that she'd taken a worker from her ISP company hostage. Those e-mails were the only thing that made her happy, and now they'd stopped. She had nothing left.

'I didn't say you were stupid,' the repairman said.

Rosemary was angry in a way she'd never experienced before. She could feel it setting like a cancer in the pit of her gut. 'You didn't say it, no,' she said. 'But you meant it, didn't you?' When she finished her sentence the room was brilliantly still, the only sound her own breath. The repairman was looking up at her, his spectacles slipping down his nose. Before she could stop herself, she threw the hot tea over his crotch. She then stood there, amazed by her own violence, the mug limp in her hand.

'Whoa!' The repairman tried to stand, the handcuffs pulling him back down into the seat. 'What are you doing, you mad bitch?' he said, his free hand going to the wet patch on his trousers. He tugged at the material, trying to pull it away from his skin, his eyes wide with shock. 'You're not right,' he said, flailing around in the chair. 'That tea is boiling hot. It's burning. I only told you those things for your own safety. I'm burning here. You have to let me go.' He crossed and uncrossed his legs, like a child who needed the toilet.

Rosemary laughed. 'No,' she said. 'You've got to fix my connection first.'

'Jesus suffering Christ!' he said. 'What's the matter with you? Is it your time of the month, or what?'

'Not that old chestnut?' Rosemary said, grinning. 'I thought you might have come up with something a bit more original.' Suddenly she was shouting again, her voice going from nought to sixty in under a second. 'Like fixing my fucking Internet!' She turned and stomped out of the room.

'Shit!' Aaron thought. 'Why did I have to say that?' He knew it pissed them off. He used to say it to his wife, and she'd left him. He was scared of what this woman was going to do next. He could hear her footsteps on the floor above him, stamping around. He felt the contour of his mobile phone through the material of his jacket. But he couldn't dial 999, not without fixing the connection. It would be too obvious that she'd been conned.

He reached for the miniature screwdriver on the floor. He wheeled the chair over to the socket, dragging it with his feet. He held the screwdriver in his left hand, supporting his wrist with his right. He shook as he tried to wedge the tip of it into the nook of the tiny screw. It kept falling out. He pushed further into the corner, the arm of the chair jammed against the wall. He could hear the woman shouting, her words muffled, as he worked the screw anti-clockwise. When the screw couldn't go any further, he pulled the screwdriver away, the shoulder of his bound arm aching. He should have done this in the first place. The other boys never told him that she was a nut job.

The tea had turned cold now, and his trousers were clinging to his thighs. He saw a small green light on the dongle begin to flash. That was probably it. He was connected. Just to make sure, he went back to the socket and tried to tighten the other screw but it was already wound as tight as it could go. He moved over to the desk and tried to work the mouse with his left hand, the arrow thrashing all over the screen. The woman was on her way down the stairs. He took a deep breath, paused, and then started again. He directed the arrow to the start box in the bottom left corner, instructing the computer to restart. He moved back to his original position, the screwdriver hidden between his soaked thighs.

The woman dropped a roll of brown parcel tape on the desk with a thud.

'It's done,' Aaron said. 'It's connected.'

She ignored him. She was fiddling with something in her hand. Aaron bobbed around in the chair, trying to see what it was. It was a box of Tampax. She took two tampons out and then picked the spool of tape up, dropping it on to her arm like a bracelet. She came towards him.

'I said it's done,' he said, holding his free arm up, trying to ward her off. She slapped his arm down. She tried to sit on Aaron's lap. He moved the chair with his feet, dodging her. 'I said it's done!' he shouted. He reached for the screwdriver and held it in front of him, the handle gripped in his fingers. The woman prised it from his hand and threw it over her shoulder. It landed with a tap on the hallway floor.

She grabbed his hand and tried to push it down on to the arm of the chair. He managed to pull it away. He trapped it beneath his left leg. The woman straddled him.

Behind them the computer was starting up with a fanfare. 'It's connected!' Aaron said. 'Look, take a look. You can let me go.'

The woman pushed all of her weight down on to his thighs. 'I'm sorry but I don't believe you,' she said. 'Must be my time of the month. It makes me a bit cynical.' She held a tampon between her thumb and forefinger and tried to push it into his mouth. 'No,' he said, turning his head this way and that, trying to avoid it. A boy at school with him had had to be rushed to casualty with a tampon trapped in his throat. He'd found it in the yard and swallowed it, thinking he could pull it back out by its string. But tampons expanded in water. He couldn't breathe, and he turned blue.

The woman pinched at his chin, trying to hold his face still.

'No!' he said, speaking without fully parting his lips. 'Come on, I did my job. Don't do anything silly now. You can let me go.' He wriggled, trying to fight her off, but she was much stronger than him. She lodged the tampon between his lips and drove it in with her forefinger. Aaron could feel the cotton wool, dry and fluffy against his tongue. He tried to bite down on it but the sensation was ghastly. He hated cotton wool. He retched and she stopped pushing. The tampon was loose in his mouth, balancing on his tongue. He bit down on the string to stop it travelling any closer to his throat.

'This isn't silly,' she said, her voice high and chirpy, the way women talked to babies. 'You know what was though, don't you?'

Aaron nodded. There wasn't much else he could do.

She took the second tampon and roughly thrust it into his mouth. Again he managed to catch it with the string before it got too close to his throat. 'There we are!' she said. She took the roll of parcel tape from her wrist and gripped its edge, a thick strand coming away with a rip. She slapped it over his mouth.

The woman stood up and inspected him, smiling proudly at her handiwork. 'Do you want a biscuit now?' she said, stepping backwards. 'You have to try my Viennese Whirls. I make the shortbread myself.' As she turned her back on him, Aaron pulled his free hand from underneath himself. He reached for the tape covering his mouth and grabbed at a corner, preparing to pluck it away. The weight of his mobile phone was burning a hole in his pocket. The woman heard him shuffling. She turned around and caught his hand. She held his wrist with both hands and pushed his forearm down on to the leather arm of the chair. She sat on it while she pulled the end of the parcel tape from the roll, the tape making a loud screeching noise as the stickiness gave way. She wound it around his arm several times. 'No!' Aaron tried to yell, his voice muted by the wadding in his mouth. He had no way of fighting back now.

The woman checked that the tape on his mouth was still secure, slapping it lightly a few times. 'There, there,' she said. 'Biscuit time. You love a biscuit, don't you, you repairmen?'

'Hmmm,' Aaron said, nodding at the monitor. He was trying to alert her to the Internet icon on the bottom left side of the screen. It was flickering, showing that it was connected.

The woman ignored the gesture. 'I'm sorry,' she said. She waved her hand around her face. 'I can't hear you. You've got tape over your mouth.' She took a biscuit from the plate and carried it to him. She held it in front of his mouth for a moment and then pushed it against the tape, the cream and jam smearing out of its sides. She flicked the top off the biscuit and then slapped it down on to Aaron's cheek. She rolled it over his face like a child pushing a toy car along a grid. He could feel the thick band of jam smearing across his skin, the buttercream getting caught among the stubble on his jaws.

Soon it was clogging every space on his face. He could feel the grittiness of the crumbs in his ear canals. There was buttercream stuffed in his nostrils. There was burgundy-coloured jam smeared on the lenses of his glasses. He couldn't see anything. All he could smell was its sickly sweet aroma, caught at the back of his throat. He felt like a fly with its wings pulled, trapped in a can of Coke. And his legs were dead from the woman sitting on them. He was so aggravated he began to cry.

'What's the matter?' Rosemary said as she noticed a tear snaking down through the yellowy buttercream spread on the repairman's face. She lifted his spectacles up and set them on top of his head. 'It's not blood. It's only jam.' She wiped a dollop of jam from under his eye with the edge of her fingertip. She put it into her mouth, the sugar tingling at her taste buds. 'See?'

The repairman was staring hard at her, his

irises golden. The two blue tampon threads were dangling out of the brown tape like tails. She realised that he couldn't answer her with his mouth taped up like that, and very suddenly all the fun had trickled out of the situation. She jumped out of his lap and stood looking down at him. 'This is grievous bodily harm, isn't it?' she said. The repairman nodded. Rosemary glanced around the room, at the roll of brown tape and the puddle of cold tea on the floor. What was she going to do now? She had to kill him or let him go.

'Bloody hell,' she said, the consequence of her actions dawning on her like thunder. She peeked at the repairman and a whimper came from the back of her throat. 'I'm sorry,' she said. 'I'm sorry.'

Chapter Seven
Escape

Behind them the front door was opening. The handle was being pressed down. Somebody was coming in. The repairman looked up expectantly. 'Shhh!' Rosemary said, glaring at him. She pressed her index finger against her lips. He blinked and then nodded. She moved towards the office door and peeked outside. Her son was in the hallway, his schoolbag on his shoulder.

'Danny!' she said, voice frantic. 'What are you doing home?' She squeezed out into the hallway, closing the door behind her. She stood in front of it, guarding the office.

'Study period,' Daniel said. He noticed the screwdriver on the floor. 'What's this?' he said. He frowned as he stooped to pick it up. He handed it to his mother.

'Oh, nothing,' she said. 'Thanks.' She quickly turned, opened the office door, and threw the screwdriver on to her desk. She flicked the light switch off and then slammed the door closed again. She stood in the doorway, grinning at her son, hands pressed protectively on her hips.

'Are you OK, Mum?' Daniel said. He was trying to look past her, through the wooden panels of the door.

'Fine!' Rosemary said. 'I'm absolutely fine.' She reached up and ruffled her son's dark hair. It was stiff and tacky with hair gel. Daniel moved away from his mother's touch. Rosemary wiped her fingers on the thigh of her jeans. 'Well, let's get you something to eat,' she said. She pointed at the kitchen door, expecting her son to move towards it. He didn't budge. 'Come on, you must be hungry.' She pushed him in front of her, following him down the narrow hall.

'How was school?' she said, as she opened the fridge door.

Danny sat at the dining table, still wearing his padded jacket. He rolled his eyes. 'It was school,' he said, shrugging. 'What do you expect me to say?'

Rosemary put a block of cheese, an onion, and a cucumber down on the worktop. She reached into the cupboard for a chopping board. 'I expect you to tell me what subjects you had. I expect you to tell me how your revision is going.' She took a knife from the cutlery drawer and lopped the end of the onion off.

'Maths and English,' Daniel said. 'That's what I have every Thursday morning.' Rosemary peeled the onion at arm's length, dropping the flakes of papery skin into a small pile on the worktop next to her. 'But you don't usually have a study period,' she said. 'Are you telling me the truth about that?'

'Yes!' Daniel said, offended. 'Do you think I'm stupid or something? I know you'd ring the school. It's our chemistry teacher. He's off sick. They couldn't get someone to take his place in time.' He stood up and dropped his bag on the surface of the table. He unzipped it and rummaged around inside. He pulled a sealed letter out. 'Can I get a stamp from your office?' he said.

'No!' Rosemary stood still, the paring knife in her hand. 'Get it later. Help me with this sandwich for a minute. Come on, come and butter the bread.' She waited until Daniel had put the letter down on the table and joined her at the worktop before she started cutting again. 'What's it for anyway?' she said.

Daniel took four slices of bread out of the bin and laid them on the counter. 'It's just an application form,' he said, 'for a Christmas job at the supermarket.' As he opened the carton of margarine, he could feel a strange energy coming from his mother. She was tense as a coiled spring, her hands shaking. He noticed a jam stain on the shoulder of her blouse, two seeds clinging to the material, the red liquid soaking in. 'What's that?' he said.

His mother jumped, her knife catching the tip of her thumb. 'What?' she said, twisting around to look at him, her thumb going to her mouth.

'There's a stain on your blouse.' As he spoke he saw the dark mascara ringed around her eyes. 'Have you been crying, Mum?'

Rosemary shook her head. 'It's the onion,' she said, pointing at it. 'Get me a plaster please, Danny. There are some blue ones in the First Aid case.' She ripped a square piece of kitchen roll from the holder and held it over her thumb. Daniel was still standing in the middle of the kitchen, staring at her. 'In the second cabinet,' she said, 'third shelf, quickly!'

Danny put the case down on the worktop and toyed with the plastic catch. 'It's a First Aid case,' he said. 'Why is it so hard to open?'

His mother pushed him out of the way and located a plaster. She wound it around her finger. Daniel noticed that there was jam under her fingernails as well. 'Hang on,' he said, his head tilted, 'wasn't the ISP guy coming to fix the connection today?'

Rosemary was still.

'I think I saw his van outside,' Danny said.

'Oh, the repairman?' Rosemary said. 'Yes, he's in there now. He's having a few problems. The line is faulty. Best to leave him be for a while.'

'But you turned the light out,' Danny said.

'No I didn't,' Rosemary said. 'I passed him his screwdriver. He must have dropped it.' She turned back to the sandwich, pulling the cover from the cucumber.

'You did,' Danny said. 'I saw you. You turned the light off.'

Outside, in the middle of the cul-de-sac, Aaron sat tied to the leather chair. He was waiting for someone to notice him. His glasses had fallen from the top of his head in the rush to escape. They'd landed in front of his eyes, the lenses still covered in jam. All he could see was the dirty fish-tank light of the outdoors, like being buried in a big jar of Vaseline. The bird song was muffled. The cold breeze bit at the insides of his thighs. The trousers were stuck to him like a fourth layer of skin.

71

He tried not to think about the damage to his skin. Instead he listened to what he could hear, or at least what he thought he could, car tyres whipping on tarmac, children playing in a park. The source of the noise seemed to come from a distance and those two hours bound up in a windowless room had confused his senses. He couldn't remember where the entrance to the cul-de-sac was. He was afraid to wheel the chair any further across the street in case he planted himself in the middle of the nearby dual carriageway, but he knew that very soon that woman was going to realise that he was gone.

It was like one of those nightmares where, while being pursued by some mad axe-man, your body became completely paralysed. But the mad axe-man was a woman, and Aaron wasn't asleep. A new overwhelming sense of frustration attacked him and he pulled at the handcuffs. By now his wrist was so swollen he wasn't able to measure the strength of the metal. All he could feel was the stinging of his skin.

He felt so bloody stupid! He had attended many courses designed to teach him how to deal with these situations. Anyone who spent most of their working lives visiting members of the public needed to risk-assess the property, as well as the client, on arrival. He remembered some of the questions on the official check list. Does the customer appear to be under the influence of alcohol or drugs? Does the property appear to be a dangerous environment? For example, is there any evidence of drug paraphernalia (needles) or dangerous weapons (knives) present? Are all pets, particularly guard dogs, locked securely in another room? He had been very aware of these sorts of issues when he did work on sink estates but this was a wealthy area of the city and nothing had seemed out of place. The woman had been slightly irritable, but well spoken and well dressed. Everything had seemed ordinary until it was too late.

He had realised he had a chance to escape the moment the woman turned the light off. She didn't want her son to know that he was there. That meant she had to keep her son busy for a period of time. Aaron had dragged the chair across the floor with the soles of his feet, as if pushing a skateboard. The door handle was at waist height. Luckily it was a handle, not a knob, and he was able to push it down with his elbow. The door burst open with an abrupt pop and he sat under the frame for a few seconds, wondering if the woman, or the boy, could hear or see him. They were at the back of the house and they were talking, but Aaron couldn't hear what they were saying. He heard them the way he heard his music while lying in the bath, a non-stop drone. The stifled sound seemed to continue without pause, so he carried on along the hallway, the plastic wheels scraping against the laminate floor.

In his head he said a prayer. 'Please God, let me make it out of here alive. If I get to the front door undetected, I promise I'll never dupe another customer for an extra bit of cash.' What do I need money for anyway, he thought, I only spend it on computer games. When he reached the front door, he was able to stand for a moment and lift the chair over the threshold. As he blindly made his way across the drive and over the kerb, he kept repeating the prayer. 'I'll never dupe a customer for any extra cash ever again. I promise, I promise, I promise.'

Now Aaron felt a hand pressing on his shoulder. 'Are you all right?' It was a woman's voice. The urgent need to identify who it belonged to forced Aaron to shake his head until his glasses fell from his face. They landed on the ground with a tinny rattle.

An elderly woman was leaning down in front of him, frowning. He pointed at the tape on his mouth, asking the woman to remove it. The woman took the corner of the tape. Aaron nodded hard, encouraging her. It came away with one pull. He spat the tampons out and they landed on the ground next to the old woman's pink slippers. She stared at them with worry. 'Just a practical joke,' Aaron said, taking a gulp of the delicious new air. 'Can you help me cut myself free? My keys are in my pocket here.' He thrust his chest out, showing the woman his breast pocket. 'There are scissors and bolt cutters in the van.'

'Shouldn't I ring 999?' the old woman said.

'No,' Aaron said. He couldn't risk involving the police. There'd be an investigation into the incident. They'd ask him why the connection had taken such a long time to repair. They'd ask him why he hadn't rung them earlier. They would ask all sorts of questions. 'I'm fine,' he said. 'It was just a joke.' He cocked his head at the bloated tampons on the ground. 'I'm getting married at the weekend,' he said. 'It was my stag party last night.'

The old woman looked unsure. She reached towards his pocket but then hesitated, her soft, crinkled fingers frozen in mid-air. 'You're not playing a trick on me?' she said. Aaron shook his head, eyes fervent. No more tricks. He felt her fingers fumbling against his chest. He heard the clatter of his keys as she lifted them out.

Daniel walked carefully towards the office, his job application seized in his hand.

'Wait,' Rosemary said, following him, the paring knife gripped in her fist. She tapped his shoulder blade to try to slow his pace, but he continued anyway along the hall. 'It's not what it looks like,' she said.

The office door was wide open. Danny reached around the frame and turned the light switch on. 'There's nobody here,' he said, puzzled. Rosemary squinted over his shoulder. The room was empty. The miniature screwdriver was on the floor, next to the upturned, jam-stained plate. The mug sat innocently on the desk. There was a faint, electrical snore from the PC, the monitor blank. Daniel turned to look at his mother.

Rosemary shrugged. 'He must have popped out for a tool,' she said. 'Unless he's finished. Is the Internet connected?' She pushed past her son and went to the computer. She pressed the space key on the keyboard and the screensaver started up with a photo of the Eiffel Tower. I should change that screensaver, she thought, too much of a giveaway. She leaned against the desk and pressed the space bar a second time. When the desktop appeared, she saw the Internet icon at the bottom left of the monitor. It was flashing bright green. 'I think it's done,' she said excitedly. She double-clicked on the purple and red ISP emblem.

Daniel picked up the plate and put it down on the desk. He picked up the screwdriver too. 'What did you mean when you said it isn't what it looks like?' he said.

Rosemary was staring at the screen, her body bent over the keyboard, her elbows on the desk. 'What?' she said, voice prickly.

'That's what you said,' Daniel said. 'You said, "It's not what it looks like." Are you having an affair with the Internet man, Mum?' He was rummaging around in the drawer looking for the book of first-class stamps.

Rosemary laughed. 'Me? An affair?' she said. 'Who would I have an affair with? I hardly leave the house!'

'But that Internet guy is here all the time!' There was a playful quality to his voice. He was joking.

'Don't be ridiculous, Danny,' she said. From

the corner of her eye she could see that he was holding a piece of paper with her spidery handwriting on it.

'What's this?' he said. He held it up to the light. 'Oranges, for Cézanne, are more than just juicy fruits,' he read, his eyebrows knitted into a squint. 'Heavier than reality, by far, they are dense geometric forms, individual beings, symbols of Eden or perhaps eternity. In this great counting game, the picture is more than the sum of its parts.' They were the notes Rosemary had made at the National Museum, according to André's instructions on how to look at art.

She plucked the paper out of her son's hand and glanced at it briefly. 'Can't remember,' she said. 'Might have been some translation work I did once for a gallery.' She scrunched the paper into a ball and flicked it into the wastebasket.

'I like Paul Cézanne,' Danny said unexpectedly.

'Do you?' Rosemary said.

'Yeah, I saw that *Still Life with Apples and Teapot* one at the museum. Dad took us there a few months ago, one night when you were working late. He liked it as well. He misses you, Mum. He doesn't like it when you work late. He takes extra clients on just for something to do.'

Rosemary stared at her son's face, wondering if he was telling the truth, or trying to catch her out. He was standing next to her, his elbows leaning on the desk. He slowly stuck the stamp on the envelope, making sure that the edges were precise, his tongue poked out in concentration. His face was a perfect blend of her and her husband. He had his father's broad nose, and her blue, emotion-filled eyes.

'Really?' Rosemary said. 'I thought it was the other way around.'

'That's what he told me,' Danny said.

Rosemary turned back to the screen. She quickly typed her password into the space provided. Her e-mail inbox opened quickly. Unread messages 0. Spam messages 47. It was what she had come to expect. She closed it again.

'Hey, Mum,' Danny said, glancing around the room. 'Where's your chair?' Before she could think of an answer, he was out of the room, heading towards the post-box at the entrance to the cul-de-sac. She followed him to the front door.

Her computer chair was in the middle of the road, the parcel tape still sticking to its arm. The repairman was standing next to his white cab, the door open, wiping his face with a cloth. The broken handcuffs were still attached to his wrist. He glanced at her before stepping into his cab.

Aaron could see the woman in his windscreen mirror. She was standing on the doorstep with her son, their voices the same muffled drone he'd heard from the kitchen. His heart was thumping, but he fought the urge to turn the key. He was safe now. His mobile phone was on the dashboard. The old woman who had snipped the handcuffs with his bolt cutter was standing on her own doorstep on the other side of the street, still baffled by the incident.

He leaned down in the seat and lifted the waist of his trousers, gingerly unzipping the fly. He pulled the material away from his skin, and it came away without any pain. He lifted the elastic of his underpants and squinted down inside. His skin was flamingo pink, clashing with the dark mound of his pubic hair. He touched it lightly, expecting some of it to come away on his fingers. It didn't. There was a sudden knock on his window. The woman's face was pressed up against the glass. He jumped. He pulled his trousers up.

'You're not going to go to the police, are you?' she said, shouting, her knuckles rapping on the glass. Aaron put his seatbelt on and started the engine. As he did the woman became more frantic. 'Please?' she said. 'Don't go to the police. It was a mistake. I didn't mean anything by it. I'm sorry.'

Aaron forced himself to look into her eyes. They were the same eyes he'd seen in the photograph in her office, happy but tinted with a spongy sadness.

'Are you?' she said. 'Please don't.'

Aaron put the van into first. He looked ahead. Let her stew, he thought.

Quick Reads

Books in the Quick Reads series

Quick Reads

We Won the Lottery
Real Life Winner Stories
Danny Buckland

Accent Press

A short, sharp shot of excitement

Fancy cars, big houses and dream holidays are all top of the wish list for the people whose lives are changed by a £1 winning lottery ticket. But what about buying a boob job for your sister or giving away holidays to children with cancer?

For the first time five winners share the details of their shopping sprees. They talk about the highs and lows of their lives after they became millionaires. *We Won the Lottery* also goes behind the scenes at the National Lottery to reveal funny facts, the luckiest numbers, the unusual purchases and exactly what happens when you win.

Quick Reads

Team Calzaghe
Michael Pearlman

Accent Press

A short, sharp shot of excitement

Never beaten in 46 fights, Joe Calzaghe became recognised as one of the greatest sportsmen in British history after his last fight against American great Roy Jones at New York's Madison Square Garden.

The man behind his success is father and mentor Enzo Calzaghe, who has produced four world champions from his tiny south Wales gym.

Team Calzaghe explores the success of the Calzaghe boxing family, which includes Enzo Maccarinelli, Bradley Pryce, Gary Lockett and Gavin Rees.

It also lifts the lid on the boxers' battles with booze, bulimia and the authorities as the Calzaghes defied their critics to rule the boxing world.

Quick Reads

Random Thoughts
Chris Corcoran

Accent Press

A short, sharp shot of excitement

It's all here. The story of how Radio Ga Ga ruined the greatest moment of my life as a teenager in the valleys.

How I learnt about the dangers of a toilet roll from my time on *CBeebies' Doodle Do*.
How not to climb mountains!
And the pointlessness of *Petits Filous*.

Is this total nonsense or the wisdom of a 21st century Welsh visionary? You decide and have a laugh too.

Quick Reads

Inside Out
Real life stories from behind bars

Accent Press

Brought together by their crimes, the prisoners at Parc Prison, Bridgend, share their stories of life on the other side of the security walls.

Whether they are tough criminals or teenagers in trouble for the first time, they all have one thing in common – they had a life outside.

The prisoners have put into words what it's really like doing time at Parc Prison, how they got there and their hopes for the future.

These stories of their lives before crime will surprise and move you, make you laugh and cry in equal measures!

Royalties from this book will go to Parc Prison's arts and educational fund to support creative workshops for prisoners.

Quick Reads

Black-Eyed Devils
Catrin Collier

Accent Press

One look was enough. Amy Watkins and Tom Kelly were in love. But that one look condemned them both.

'Look at Amy again and you'll return to Ireland in a box.' Amy's father is out to kill Tom.

All Tom wants is Amy and a wage that will keep them. But Tonypandy in 1911 is a dangerous place for Irish workers like Tom, who have been brought in to replace the striking miners. The miners drag them from their beds and hang them from lamp posts as a warning to those who would take their jobs.

Frightened for Amy, Tom fights to deny his heart, while Amy dreams of a future with the man she loves. But in a world of hatred, anger and violence, her dream seems impossible until a man they believed to be their enemy offers to help. But, can they trust him with their lives?

 Quick Reads

Alive and Kicking
Andy Legg

Accent Press

Andy Legg is one of the best-loved players in Welsh international football and his legendary long throw-in earned him a place in the record book.

One of a select few to play for South Wales arch-rivals Swansea City and Cardiff City, Andy played six times for Wales and more than 600 League games for Swansea, Notts County, Birmingham City, Peterborough, Reading and Cardiff.

But in 2005 his life was turned upside down when a lump in his neck turned out to be cancer. Alive and Kicking is Andy's emotional account of his treatment, his fears for his life and how the messages of support from his fans gave him the strength to fight on and return to the game.

Quick Reads

In at the Deep End
From Barry to Beijing
David Davies

Accent Press

As he was carried off on a stretcher at the Olympics in Beijing, Welsh swimmer David Davies was celebrating his success. He'd won a silver medal in one of the toughest races in the Olympics.

He also won a place in British swimming history as the first male swimmer to win medals at two consecutive Olympic Games in over thirty years.

In At The Deep End: From Barry To Beijing is David's own story of the highs and lows of his career. How a lanky schoolboy from Barry made the swimming world sit up and take notice. From his first success at the Commonwealth Games at the age of 17, he has gone on to win medals at every major championship. And he's still only 24.

About the Author

Photo: Huw John

Rachel Trezise was born in the Rhondda Valley in 1978. She studied at Glamorgan and Limerick Universities. Her first novel *In and Out of the Goldfish Bowl* was a winner of the Orange Futures Prize. Her first collection of short fiction *Fresh Apples* won the EDS Dylan Thomas Prize. Her documentary about Welsh rock band Midasuno, *Dial M for Merthyr*, was published in 2007. Her second novel *Sixteen Shades of Crazy* will be published by HarperCollins in 2010.